Bob the Builder

Run-Away Roley

by Alison Inches

illustrated by Art Ellis

SCHOLASTIC INC.

New York Toronto London Auckland Sydney
Mexico City New Delhi Hong Kong Buenos Aires

Based upon the television series *Bob the Builder*™
created by HIT Entertainment PLC and Keith Chapman,
with thanks to HOT Animation 🔶, as seen on Nick Jr.®

No part of this publication may be reproduced in whole or in part, or stored in a
retrieval system, or transmitted in any form or by any means, electronic,
mechanical, photocopying, recording, or otherwise, without written permission of
the publisher. For information regarding permission, write to Simon Spotlight,
an imprint of Simon & Schuster Children's Publishing Division,
1230 Avenue of the Americas, New York, NY 10020.

ISBN 0-439-41881-X

12 11 10 9 8 7 6 5 4 3 2 1   2 3 4 5 6 7/0

Printed in the U.S.A.

First Scholastic printing, September 2002

Honk, shoo! Honk, shoo!

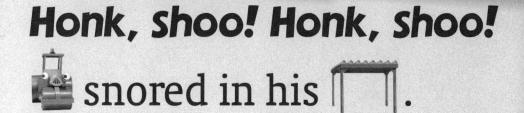 snored in his .

ROLEY   GARAGE

It had been a long day.

When the sun came up,  was still sleeping.

ROLEY

Then  began to roll and snore.  was sleep-rolling!

He rolled toward  PILCHARD.

"**Meow!**" said PILCHARD.

But ROLEY kept rolling.

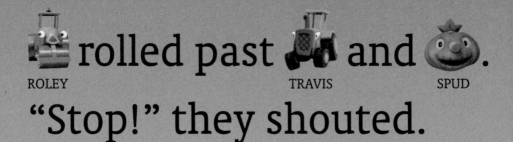

ROLEY rolled past TRAVIS and SPUD.

"Stop!" they shouted.

But  kept rolling.

ROLEY

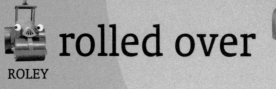 rolled over .

ROLEY   MAILBOXES

Crash!

And 🗑🗑.
GARBAGE CANS

Bang!

ROLEY rolled over **TRAFFIC CONES**. **Splat!**

And a . **Bonk!**

LAMPPOST

even rolled into a ▓▓▓▓.

ROLEY   FENCE

Whack!

Then  rolled straight

ROLEY

toward a big ____ !

HOLE

BOB came running.

"Look out!" BOB cried.
But ROLEY kept rolling.

 put over

BOB PLANKS

the .

HOLE

Then he put his hands over his eyes.

"I can't look!" said.

BOB

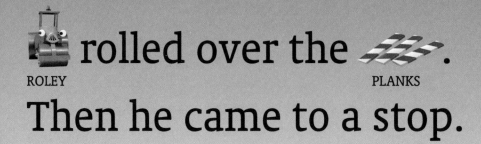 rolled over the .

Then he came to a stop.

"  made it!" said  .

ROLEY   BOB

But  did not wake up.

ROLEY

"It is getting late. We need  to tow  home," said .

LOFTY

ROLEY

BOB

"Hooray!" said the machines when ROLEY got home.

opened his eyes.
"Hi!" he said. "I had a good rest. Let's rock and roll!"

ROLEY

But everyone was ready for bed.

"Good night, !"
said the machines.
Then they began
to snore.

Honk, shoo!

Honk, shoo!